ARI THE BRAVE'S

JUNGLE JOURNEY

Scan the QR code for a read aloud, narrated by Jaclyn Marino.

Rainbow Wings
Publishing, LLC

Written by
Krystal Wallick

Illustrated by
Sarah Nettuno

FROM THE AUTHOR:

For the real-life Ari, whose journey in the NICU inspired this story.
For the NICU team at Bethesda Hospital in Boynton Beach, FL, who saved his life.
And for Ari's dad and big sisters, who braved this journey with us.

Thank you to Anabelle Wallick, Benjamin Runnebaum,
Max Runnebaum, and Avery Langer for inspiring some of the
unusual animals you will find throughout the book.

FROM THE ILLUSTRATOR:

Many thanks to my husband, John Aaron, my family and friends, and God for
helping me arrive where I am today as an illustrator of very important stories.

ARI THE BRAVE'S JUNGLE JOURNEY

RAINBOW WINGS PUBLISHING LLC books are available from your favorite bookseller
or from www.rainbowwingspublishing.com

Hardcover ISBN: 978-1-7363828-0-6
Paperback ISBN: 978-1-7363828-1-3
Ebook ISBN: 978-1-7363828-2-0

Library of Congress Control Number: 2021913078
Cataloging in Publication data on file with the publisher.

Cover and Layout Design: Rachel Thomaier

Printed in the USA

10 9 8 7 6 5 4 3 2 1

"Why do I have to stay at the hospital, Mom?"

"Well, Ari," says Mom, "there's a small problem with your lungs, and Dr. Jo and the nurses are going to fix it."

"You mean my breathing machines, Mom?"

"Yes, that's right. Your lungs are the machines that make your body breathe."

"Will I need surgery?"

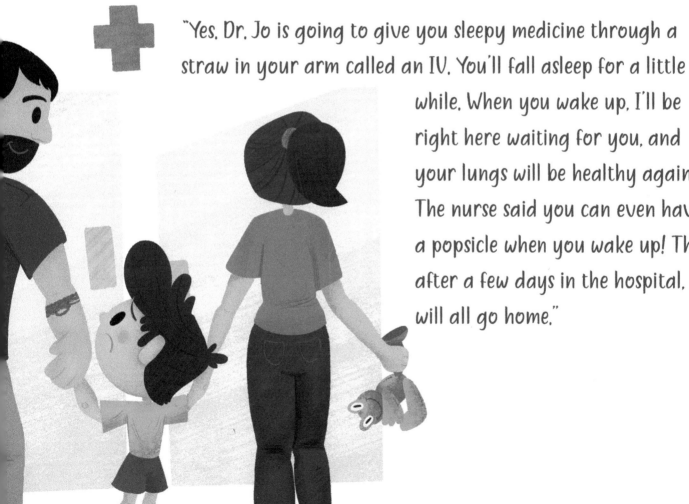

"Yes, Dr. Jo is going to give you sleepy medicine through a straw in your arm called an IV. You'll fall asleep for a little while. When you wake up, I'll be right here waiting for you, and your lungs will be healthy again. The nurse said you can even have a popsicle when you wake up! Then, after a few days in the hospital, we will all go home."

1

Not knowing what's going to happen is scary for Ari, so he decides to turn his hospital visit into an adventure. **"I'LL PRETEND THAT I'M GOING TO A BIG JUNGLE INSTEAD OF HAVING SURGERY!"** he announces.

But when they arrive in the hospital room, Ari feels a little nervous.

"IT'S NORMAL TO FEEL NERVOUS. BUT REMEMBER,

you are **BRAVE.**

You are **STRONG.**

You can **DO THIS!"** says Mom.

2   **"YES, I CAN!"** Ari answers boldly. The nurses all smile.

3

As Ari drifts off to sleep, he pretends to be deep in the jungle.

He sees tall trees and vines growing high up on the hospital walls.
Green grass grows over the checkered floor. His tubes and wires turn
to pesky spiderwebs. He shoos the spiders away.

The bright lights of the operating room turn into the shining sun. The sounds of the doctors and nurses rushing around become monkeys swinging through the treetops. Ari remembers his mom's words and says to himself.

"I AM BRAVE.

I AM STRONG.

I CAN DO THIS!"

As Ari explores his new jungle, he suddenly hears a frightening sound. He turns around and . . . WHAT? A giant rhinoceros with a great big horn shoots a blazing ball of fire out of his nose. **"YIKES! SINCE WHEN DO RHINOS BLOW FIRE?"** Ari shouts.

He quickly jumps out of the way. Even though Ari is scared, he wants to prove how brave and strong he can be. **"YOU ARE NO MATCH FOR ME, MR. RHINOCEROS!"** he says.

6

Ari looks around, and sees a sword hidden in the bushes.

"UGH, THOSE PESKY SPIDER WEBS ARE ALL OVER THE BUSHES,"

he moans. Ari bravely shoos the spiders away . . . then reaches for the sword, raises it high above his head and begins swinging. He yells,

"I AM BRAVE. I AM STRONG. I CAN DO THIS!"

The rhinoceros squeals and runs away. Phew! **"ONE CHALLENGE DOWN,"** Ari says. **"I CAN DO THIS!"**

7

Ari continues his journey. He meets other small and very unusual creatures. One of the creatures is very friendly. "HI, I'M CINDY," says a super-fluffy, teeny-tiny miniature cheetah.

"CAN I JOIN YOU ON YOUR ADVENTURE?"

"OF COURSE!" says Ari.

9

Ari and Cindy climb trees. They build forts out of sticks and leaves. They watch the monkeys swinging through the treetops and practice sword tricks …

… all while trying to avoid those pesky spiderwebs.

But even though he is having fun, Ari is still a little afraid of what else might be lurking in the jungle. He will be careful.

"I AM BRAVE. I AM STRONG. I CAN DO THIS!" he says to Cindy.

12

Cindy and Ari
WALK
and
WALK
and
WALK.

13

Soon, they come to a river.

"HEY, SOMEONE LEFT A CANOE HERE!" Ari shouts as he hops in for a ride.

"COME ON, CINDY. LET'S SEE WHERE THIS RIVER GOES. OH NO! THERE ARE EVEN SPIDERWEBS IN THIS CANOE."

Cindy helps Ari shoo away the spiderwebs, and they start to paddle.

14

15

After rowing for what seems like forever, they come across a waterfall.
The water starts rushing

HARDER

and **LOUDER**

and **FASTER.**

"**I HAVE A BAD FEELING ABOUT THIS,**" says Ari.

Cindy agrees and says, "LET'S FIND A SAFE PLACE TO DOCK."

17

But as they are heading back to shore, a huge
purple octopus rises out of the water, nearly
flipping their canoe.

Ari shouts, "WHAT? HOW DID AN OCTOPUS GET IN A RIVER?"

Ari is terrified, but he knows that with his sword and Cindy by his side, he
18   can conquer this. After all, he already beat a fire-breathing rhinoceros.

The octopus swings its tentacles and makes a
BIG
WHOPPING
SPLASH!

The waves become so rough that Ari can barely hold on any longer.

He grabs tight onto Cindy for support, Cindy lets out a great big roar and reminds Ari,
"YOU ARE BRAVE. YOU ARE STRONG. YOU CAN DO THIS." 19

Ari takes a deep breath, raises the sword above his head, and begins swinging.

Just as before, he shouts,
"I AM BRAVE.

I AM STRONG.

I CAN DO THIS!"

20

The octopus gives one final flip of a big purple tentacle and disappears way down into the water.

GONE!

"WOOHOO!" Ari and Cindy cheer. Ari knows now that even though he was afraid and nervous before, he can do anything.

21

Ari and Cindy quickly find a safe spot on the shore.
When Ari starts to hear a voice in the distance.
It's a familiar voice, and it's getting **LOUDER** and **LOUDER**,

He can see his mom waiting for him! They dock, and Ari
runs into her arms. He knows he is finally safe.

Ari tells her, "**MAMA, YOU'LL NEVER BELIEVE IT!**"

"I battled a fire-breathing **RHINOCEROS** and an enormous **OCTOPUS. I WAS SO BRAVE AND STRONG! I DID IT!**"

Giggling, she says to him, "I think you've had enough adventure."

Ari hides his sword under some bushes. He is surprised to find that there are no pesky spiderwebs in his way. **"GOODBYE, CINDY. I'LL MISS YOU,"** he says, giving her a hug and a pat on the head.

24

When Ari opens his eyes, he's no longer in the jungle. The tall trees and vines are back to white hospital walls. The green grass is back to the checkered hospital floor. The swinging monkeys are gone, and the nurses are rushing around again. Ari's parents are next to his bed.

His mom says, **"I'M PROUD OF YOU, ARI."**

"YOU WERE BRAVE.

YOU WERE STRONG.

YOU DID IT!"

Ari smiles. He did it.

TALKING TO KIDS ABOUT STAYING IN THE HOSPITAL

Sometimes, as adults, it's hard to know how children interpret different terminology. For example, they might think of a blood draw like drawing a picture or an IV flush like flushing a toilet. This may make them feel unprepared when it's time for a procedure, surgery, or hospital stay. Feeling unprepared can result in worry and anxiety. In order to help children feel brave and strong through their hospital stay, try using this kid-friendly language when talking about the hospital.

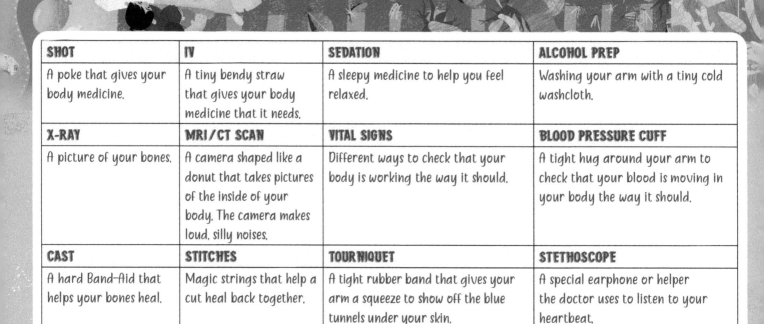

SHOT	IV	SEDATION	ALCOHOL PREP
A poke that gives your body medicine.	A tiny bendy straw that gives your body medicine that it needs.	A sleepy medicine to help you feel relaxed.	Washing your arm with a tiny cold washcloth.
X-RAY	**MRI/CT SCAN**	**VITAL SIGNS**	**BLOOD PRESSURE CUFF**
A picture of your bones.	A camera shaped like a donut that takes pictures of the inside of your body. The camera makes loud, silly noises.	Different ways to check that your body is working the way it should.	A tight hug around your arm to check that your blood is moving in your body the way it should.
CAST	**STITCHES**	**TOURNIQUET**	**STETHOSCOPE**
A hard Band-Aid that helps your bones heal.	Magic strings that help a cut heal back together.	A tight rubber band that gives your arm a squeeze to show off the blue tunnels under your skin.	A special earphone or helper the doctor uses to listen to your heartbeat.
IMMUNIZATION	**VEIN**	**RADIOLOGY DYE**	**SURGERY**
A shot that is a shield to protect your body from getting sick.	Little blue tunnels under your skin that move your blood all through your body.	Silly water that goes through your straw and into your tunnels to help your blood light up so we can take pictures of your blood. We call it silly water because kids have said it makes them feel silly.	You will fall asleep by getting sleepy medicine through an IV or sleepy air through a mask so that the doctors can fix a part of your body that is hurt.

ADDITIONAL RESOURCES FOR HELPING CHILDREN COPE WITH MEDICAL ISSUES:

www.childlifepodcast.com   www.kidshealth.org   www.tinydocs.co   www.childlifecooperative.com

ABOUT THE AUTHOR

Krystal Wallick is an author, teacher, mental health counselor, and mom of three. Her writing journey began after her son's life-threatening medical diagnosis. She hopes that her writing can help children be brave and resilient through challenging situations. When Krystal is not writing amazing adventures for other children, she enjoys her career as an instructional facilitator to mental health professionals and teachers in her public school district. Krystal loves having her own adventures with her husband and three young children at the beach, parks, and zoos in South Florida, where they live with two dogs and two cats.

ABOUT THE ILLUSTRATOR

Sarah Nettuno is a dreamer by day and an artist by night, based out of New York. In 2014, she became a student at Savannah College of Art and Design in Savannah, GA. She graduated with a BFA in illustration! While she was in college, she did an internship at Walt Disney World and got to live out her dream of working for the mouse. She also studied abroad in Lacoste, France, during her last quarter at SCAD. She specializes in kidlit art, products, toys, board and card games, gift illustration, and anything else that's cute and fun!

HIDDEN IN THE JUNGLE

Hidden in the book are **19** frogs. Can you find them all?

Visit www.AriTheBrave.com for the answers!

What other strange creatures did you see?

LOOK FOR MORE ARI THE BRAVE BOOKS AT
WWW.ARITHEBRAVE.COM

ARI THE BRAVE SERIES

Ari the Brave's Jungle Journey: Book 1
Ari the Brave's Magic Dream Fairy: Book 2

CPSIA information can be obtained
at www.ICGtesting.com
Printed in the USA
BVHW021641100821
614091BV00008B/456